P. G. Hubert

Chip of the Old Block

P. G. Hubert

Chip of the Old Block

ISBN/EAN: 9783337376338

Printed in Europe, USA, Canada, Australia, Japan

Cover: Foto ©Andreas Hilbeck / pixelio.de

More available books at **www.hansebooks.com**

CHIP OF THE OLD BLOCK:

A Comedy, in Three Acts,

By P. G. HUBERT.

A Chip of the old Block.

Characters:

Jack Barry, [illegible]
Charles [illegible]
Joseph [illegible]
[illegible]
Madeline Barry (the Chip)
Madeline Barry, her cousin, usually called Lena.

Place London — Time 189[illegible].

Act I.

A sitting room in London lodging [illegible] with theatrical pictures [illegible], actors etc. — Foils, boxing glo[ves] [illegible] of Shakespeare — [illegible] student — Open trunk near table [illegible].

Enter Barry his arms full of [illegible] and property which he sets on [illegible].

Bar. From this day I cease to be old Jack Barry, the actor, and I become John Barry "Esq" Attorney at Law. (Puts things in trunk) Away with ye! tokens of the past. (Takes up [illegible] and wig) Ah, I'll [illegible] ing [illegible] my blue bag! Where is my bag? Ah, here it is. (Throws it on chair) (Knock) — Come in.

Enter Jovel singing.

[illegible] Hullo! Hullo! Hullo! What — in the wings?
[illegible] Oh! didn't you get my note?
[illegible] Why no.
[illegible] Didn't you see my advertisement?
[illegible] Not I, me boy.
[illegible] (takes up paper) Here it is (reads) Remo[val] — Mr John Barry takes pleasure in [illegible] his friends [illegible] that his drama[illegible] [illegible] to his new [illegible] [illegible] Street, [illegible]
[illegible]

Lov. The important document had escaped [illegible] delighted vision (sets hat on table) Well, shall we begin? "If it were done, when it is done, then it were well it were done quickly."

Bar. My dear fellow, I am sincerely sorry, but I wrote to you, upon my word I did — I wrote asking you to put off this rehearsal till to-morrow. You see (points to trunk) I am moving.

Lov. Oh, all right — all right — but what is the fun? [illegible] [illegible] Bardell versus Pickwick, [illegible] you old reprobate!

Bar. No, no — [illegible], you see, my little girl is coming home.

Lov. Oh, did not know you had one.

Bar. Yes, yes — [illegible] taken to France by her aunt when my poor wife died — quite a baby then — not three years old. She's been in one of their convents ever since — Haven't seen her for fourteen years.

Lov. Devoted parent — the child — the child! we meet at last! — must feel like a stranger.

Bar. Stranger! why man, from the time her little hands have been able to trace a line, there is not a week but I have had a letter from her, see, here they all are — Every year by itself (takes up a bundle of letters) From the few short lines printed by her baby fingers (kisses letters) to the last one, telling me she has just left Paris.

Lov. Haw — yes — very nice.

Bar. And here are her portraits, in this album (opens it) One for every year — Always taken on her birthday — that's when she left me.

Lov. Hollo! tatty, polly — what's that in her hand — a kitten?

Bar. Yes — (looks fondly)

Lov. (turns leaves) Nice little thing (with more interest) Pretty child — (eagerly) — I say (?) [illegible] Why didn't you tell us? [illegible] old dog (pokes him) Why, she is a [illegible] [illegible] [illegible]

Bar. Yes, [illegible] [illegible]

With [illegible]
rate of [illegible]
Gov. Hum [illegible]
I say [illegible]
Bar. Not if I [illegible]
Gov. Why?
Bar. My [illegible] [illegible] till [illegible] is a sort of [illegible] near [illegible].
Gov. [illegible] – "Mark where she stands" (sets his [illegible] on floor) "there – around her form [illegible] the awful circle of our solemn church! Set but a foot within that holy ground, and on thy head – yea, tho' it wore a crown – I launch the curse of Rome!"
Bar. I [illegible] you [illegible]
Gov. Now, [illegible] you know, Barry [illegible] they wouldn't cast me in [illegible] astonish'd [illegible] of [illegible].
Bar. No doubt you [illegible] (Bar [illegible])
Gov. And so you are going to star [illegible] the fair [illegible] like an old [illegible]
Bar. In the first place, she is engaged.
Gov. Oh, she is.
Bar. Yes, to her cousin – young [illegible] Oxford, sir – University man – [illegible]
Gov. Just so – regular Don –
Bar. Beside which, I don't [illegible] know a thing about the stage.
Gov. What! ashamed of the footlights.
Bar. No sir – no, I am not ashamed [illegible] profession sir – and I trust my [illegible] is not ashamed of me – but what's good enough for me – [illegible] you understand. All this (points to [illegible]) goes to Seymour Street, where I shall be glad to see my friends, but here I am John Barry Esq., a lawyer, sir, and I don't know a soul. Not a soul –
Gov. Oh, very well, as you like.

[illegible] out-
Bev. [illegible] -night
about [illegible] guard)
Bye-bye [illegible]
Bar. ([illegible]) [illegible] and the
ticket [illegible] quarter past!
Only [illegible]
my [illegible] How touching.
this [illegible] reception [illegible]
[illegible] (takes [illegible] in trunk) [illegible]
[illegible]
[illegible]
[illegible] feeling [illegible]
[illegible] of spring flowers
[illegible] out of paper and sets
[illegible] on table) Shall [illegible] per-
[illegible] Now [illegible] (takes
[illegible] motto) there's nothing
like this to give a room the most strange
[illegible] respectability. (reads) "Home
Sweet Home" Now that's a very [illegible]
appropriate [illegible] "Sweet Home" in
the [illegible] of dear [illegible]
[illegible] "Beware
of [illegible] forget
[illegible] something to
[illegible] (groans) [illegible] hang this in
[illegible] sight of dear Edward [illegible] it - takes
[illegible] motto) "We are but worms" -
[illegible] worms - hum - Well so we are -
[illegible] are - worms - never shrink from
the truth - and, there is soothing in
the thought - too because worms are
such innocent creatures - I'll put the
worms under dear Edward - Now
I think that looks just about right.
(Knock) Ah, there's the man for the
trunk. (Enter porter) All ready - 44
Seymour St the address is on the card

[illegible] Sauce [illegible]

[illegible] the cook [illegible]

[illegible]

[illegible] English from France for [illegible]

[illegible]) – [illegible] – [illegible]

[illegible] becoming – excitedly) ([illegible]

[illegible]

[illegible]

([illegible] smiles and [illegible]

[illegible] which [illegible] for [illegible]

[illegible] care [illegible]!

[illegible]

[illegible]

[illegible]

[illegible]

[illegible] drawing [illegible]

[illegible]

[illegible] I am [illegible]

[illegible]

[illegible] ([illegible]

[illegible]

[illegible]

[illegible]

– We'll never part again.

– [illegible] till [illegible]

[illegible] home and [illegible]

[illegible]

[illegible]

[illegible] & did a [illegible] – [illegible] from and this is [illegible] I have so often dreamed of.

It plain case enough.

– [illegible] it is bright to me. – your [illegible] father. (brings wine)

[illegible] you must be [illegible] tired.

[illegible] I am not a bit tired [illegible] [illegible] ([illegible]

Here I am – [illegible] for [illegible]

[illegible]

[illegible]
[illegible]
[illegible] only [illegible] change [illegible]
[illegible] from [illegible], anything [illegible]
[illegible]
[illegible] means to you
[illegible]
[illegible] your [illegible] that [illegible]
[illegible] at you [illegible] bring [illegible]
[illegible] is your [illegible]
[illegible]
[illegible]
[illegible]
[illegible] — your [illegible]
[illegible]
[illegible]
[illegible] stop [illegible]
[illegible]
[illegible]
[illegible]
[illegible]
[illegible]
[illegible]
[illegible] over [illegible]
[illegible]
[illegible]
[illegible]
[illegible] closed [illegible]
[illegible] on the stage, [illegible]
[illegible]
[illegible] nothing
[illegible] you ill?
[illegible]
[illegible] knocked [illegible]
[illegible]
[illegible]
[illegible]
[illegible] your [illegible]
[illegible]
[illegible]

[illegible] your wits! – [illegible] to [illegible] days – two whole days and you [illegible] word to say! – Don't you know [illegible] every word – for every thought [illegible] all from the very beginning

[illegible] I reached Paris at six – by rail – and [illegible] and I took a cab – and –

[illegible] Yes. –

[illegible] – And I went to [illegible] –

[illegible] – Well? –

[illegible] We had songs, and [illegible] dinner – and – and [illegible] –

[illegible] When the [illegible] what [illegible] – Madeline [illegible] – [illegible] Madeline [illegible] What [illegible]

[illegible] Madeline! [illegible] describe [illegible] of spring flowers! [illegible]

[illegible] – What – you mean –

[illegible] – I mean that [illegible] why did you [illegible] me –

[illegible] – Stop! – When I [illegible] you [illegible] [illegible] that [illegible] [illegible] speak one word of [illegible]

[illegible] – [illegible] you [illegible] stone

[illegible] I thought you [illegible] No, no, not [illegible] – [illegible] [illegible] to you [illegible] you [illegible] [illegible] this [illegible] fourteen years I have [illegible] heart and kept [illegible] [illegible] this! –

[illegible] Yes sir – yes I know –

([illegible] you know [illegible] [illegible] your [illegible] [illegible] [illegible]

[illegible] me so.
[illegible] you
[illegible]
[illegible] feelings [illegible] my heart.
[illegible] to me. [illegible]
[illegible] my face —
[illegible] if [illegible] [illegible]
[illegible] ground [illegible]
[illegible] your [illegible]
[illegible]
[illegible]
[illegible]
[illegible]
[illegible]
[illegible]
[illegible]

[illegible]
[illegible]
[illegible]
[illegible]
[illegible]
[illegible] you! [illegible]
[illegible] your [illegible]
[illegible] mean!
[illegible] to go.
[illegible] don't [illegible]
[illegible]
[illegible] face [illegible]
[illegible]
[illegible] it!
[illegible]
[illegible]
[illegible] if I [illegible]
[illegible] !
[illegible] me would [illegible]
[illegible] you [illegible] speak to [illegible]
[illegible] to [illegible]
[illegible] knows [illegible] mine?
[illegible] me! —
[illegible] will [illegible]
[illegible]

... and ...
... for go for a little while.
... save me! Pshaw! ...
... for a time, and –
Why –! Because I spoke a hasty
word or two – ...
... never mind Sir
...
... you, my boy, ...
...

... you, sir. You ...
...
... See ...
... away – ...
... am ... – Wh...
over ... she is Edward ...
O dad ...
... for my sake Charl...
... you ... case ... I
... I must ...
... get over ... we can't be
...
... mi... own
... with ...
... you – I can trust you Charl
... I trust myself –
Oh ... nonsense. Be a man – I
...
I'll stay dad – I'll stay – and yo...
... of ... never ...
...ment –
... Hush! ...
... looks
... admiringly, ...
... bome! – Not a thing ...
... bowl, ...
... the hands at the head of ...
... piece ... kept out.

[illegible] ice [illegible] wheat, papa.

[illegible] H [illegible] ---

[illegible] piece of pastry.

[illegible] getting [illegible] [illegible]

[illegible] [illegible] flatter myself the [illegible]

[illegible] [illegible] miss.

[illegible] Darling! [illegible] Knock

[illegible] [illegible] little [illegible]

[illegible] goes to dawn, returns with [illegible]

[illegible] etc. [illegible] [illegible]

[illegible] are [illegible] the [illegible]

[illegible] [illegible] — [illegible]

[illegible]

[illegible] never mind [illegible]

[illegible] us with the [illegible] [illegible]

[illegible] well what the [illegible] what are you [illegible]

[illegible]

[illegible] you [illegible] that bell, [illegible]

[illegible] [illegible] And [illegible] of my [illegible]

[illegible] [illegible] one [illegible] cage of [illegible]

[illegible] [illegible] never did — [illegible]

[illegible] to show me how —

[illegible] will do that — [illegible]

[illegible] [illegible] from us.

[illegible] is [illegible] [illegible] in [illegible]

[illegible] two lag [illegible] for [illegible]

[illegible] [illegible], make it [illegible].

[illegible] [illegible] — and for you?

[illegible] [illegible] two [illegible].

[illegible] [illegible], sweet sixteen.

[illegible] [illegible], papa nearly [illegible]

[illegible] now [illegible] in the tea — [illegible] in [illegible]

[illegible] [illegible] will do.

[illegible] [illegible] the cream

[illegible] No, no — not so much — just a [illegible]

[illegible] [illegible] [illegible]

[illegible] [illegible] won't be nice at all, [illegible]

[illegible] plenty of milk, [illegible] [illegible]

[illegible] [illegible]

[illegible] [illegible] [illegible] [illegible] [illegible]

[illegible]

[illegible] in [illegible] income

[illegible] Circuit.

[illegible]

[illegible]

M. [illegible]

[illegible]

[illegible] your [illegible] you.

M. Why I am amused - don't move - [illegible] me! (Builds) that's your cottage.

[illegible] My cottage.

M. Yes the little cottage of last night - Don't you remember? - Oh! how I love the sea! It was the first time I had ever seen the sea. How grand it was [illegible] calm, how full of [illegible] [illegible] [illegible] stretching far, far away [illegible] [illegible] it blended with the [illegible] sky. [illegible] you remember [illegible] [illegible] on the way through the [illegible] [illegible] moment [illegible] follow the [illegible] [illegible] [illegible] upon the [illegible] [illegible] - [illegible] you remember [illegible] [illegible] [illegible] path leading [illegible] [illegible] and [illegible] where you [illegible] [illegible] and the little cottage [illegible] [illegible] [illegible] dreams - [illegible] [illegible] [illegible] [illegible] - don't [illegible] [illegible] [illegible] I [illegible] [illegible] [illegible] [illegible] [illegible] [illegible] [illegible] [illegible] [illegible] [illegible]

[illegible]

[illegible]

[illegible]
. There! (claps on scarf jumps [illegible]) [illegible] looks admiringly [illegible]
. It was so kind of you, to think of me.
. And I have such a nice present for you
you'll see.
. I do hope you will like our English [illegible]
- and your new home.
. Like it! Ah, you don't know how [illegible]
the very word is to me - home, my home
I am going to be such a little house[illegible]
I am going to keep every thing so bright
[illegible] neat. (Jumps up) Let us begin!
[illegible] - Oh yes, certainly [illegible]
[illegible]
. First, [illegible] the house, and you [illegible]
[illegible] every thing, and [illegible]
[illegible] - and tell me just [illegible]
[illegible] I don't know a thing, [illegible]
[illegible] I have all [illegible] put it [illegible]
[illegible] tell me [illegible] I'll put them [illegible]
[illegible] and leave them to [illegible]
[illegible], I am not going to have [illegible]
[illegible] cups and saucers breakfast [illegible]
. Aunt [illegible] always washed [illegible]
[illegible] china [illegible], I know that [illegible]
[illegible] our best china [illegible]
[illegible] have no [illegible].
. The more reason for being [illegible]
I'll show you - [illegible]
[illegible] - then, put on [illegible]
[illegible] rest of the [illegible]
. Allow me (takes [illegible])
. Take care! you will [illegible]
cuffs - take them [illegible]
[illegible]
[illegible] water) [illegible]
[illegible] you [illegible].

[illegible] you'll wash [illegible] (She [illegible] it is one [illegible] (Brother [illegible] Mrs. but you must rub them [illegible] all to shine like mirrors. [illegible] work.)

[illegible]. How will this do?

M. I am afraid your water is not hot enough. (raises [illegible])

[illegible]. (Stopping [illegible]) [illegible] I am [illegible] water enough as it is!

M. Why, how [illegible] you [illegible] in water, I can hold my hand right in it. (She takes [illegible] hand [illegible]) Oh I [illegible] it without [illegible]

[illegible]. I beg your [illegible] to me but [illegible] to you, [illegible].

M. [illegible] away - [illegible] that cousin Edward?

[illegible]. Yes

M. What a queer dress [illegible]

Ch. It is the Oxford [illegible].

M. And how [illegible], [illegible] is not a bit like you.

[illegible]. (Bitterly) [illegible] a gentleman [illegible]

M. Why, what's the [illegible].

Ch. Nothing -

M. You look so strange and [illegible] silent - you are not a bit like [illegible]

[illegible]. You think so -

M. Why don't you talk [illegible]

[illegible]. [illegible], yes - what shall we [illegible] about?

M. Talk about! [illegible] you [illegible] night - about the [illegible] - [illegible] and sadly, [illegible] I am afraid you [illegible] getting tired of my prattle.

[illegible] - tired -

M. You know everything [illegible] I never [illegible] anything [illegible] any one except to the girls and [illegible]

[illegible] France.

[illegible] things [illegible] that [illegible] a single word to a young man.

[illegible] young ladies [illegible] in France.

[illegible] English customs! [illegible] if [illegible] were to [illegible] the sofa [illegible]

[illegible] with [illegible] improve- [illegible]

[illegible] would [illegible]

[illegible] what is the [illegible]

[illegible]

again - never! never! - and - and (half crying) I who thought we should be such friends, and who was so happy last night - but now - you - are not a bit nice - and - and I do wish papa would return (noise at door) - Ah! (Runs to door - Enter Barry - embraces her.)

Bar - Well you see I was not [illegible] (looks at her) But - what is this - tears? -

M. It is cousin Charles - Mr. Stewart, I mean - he is so strange - and cold - and - and he is so disagreeable, hateful - - -

B. Tut, tut, tut - you'll soon know him better. (Gives Ch's hand & [illegible] - Exit Ch.) He will be a true brother to you.

M. Last night he was so kind - we had such a pleasant time - and now - he will hardly speak a word, and - and - he calls me Miss Barry, and [illegible] -

B. Well, well - the boy is not himself tonight - he is not well - you must be kind to him, Madeline - You must be kind to Charley.

M. (Half crying) I meant to be so kind -

B. That's right (soothes her) - Why - you have moved the sofa, & [illegible] - and the table.

M. (Brightening up) Yes - doesn't it look well? - Oh, I am going to make [illegible] room so pretty -

B. Of course you will - it will be such another room with [illegible] - (Points to mottoes) and look at these . .

M. Oh they are lovely, but what queer letters - I cannot read it.

B. Old English - Dear Edward painted them. (reads) "Home sweet home!"

M. That is lovely!

B. Yes (reads) "A vale of tears."

M. "Tears" - what a strange idea - what does it mean?

B. Well, my dear, it means - well, tears you know - tears -

M. But it sounds so sad -

B. Yes - rather - but it is well we should

remember, you know – this life – "a vale of tears" – you know.

M. But I don't like to remember – And this one (points to last motto – tries to read) we – we – we are –

B. Oh, this one – hem – well, hem – "We are but worms!"

M. Worms! Oh, horrible! take it down, papa, please take it down.

B. But my child –

M. I could not live with that dreadful thing before my eyes – please, please, papa take it down – and take down the "vale of tears" too.

B. Certainly, my pet, if you insist (gets on chair) but –

M. And I have such a lovely thing for you. (runs out, returns with pictures) See, see, Miss Sefton and Rockville!

B. What! of the St. James!

M. Yes, yes, they were in Paris, you know, at the exposition – and I was so anxious to see an English play that aunt took me. (B. goes to table, back – stands looking on)

M. They were splendid! and I brought their portraits for you –

B. For me! (looks at pictures) Hum

M. (disappointed) Why, don't you like them?

B. Oh, they are excellent – excellent (turns them up) thank you my child, thank you

M. Did you ever see Miss Sefton?

B. Hum! yes, my dear, yes, I have seen her.

M. It was the "Lady of Lyons" one of Bulwer's plays – did you ever see the "Lady of Lyons" papa?

B. Yes, yes – I have seen the play –

M. Oh, that scene when she finds out who he is and turns upon him in scorn (recites lines tamely) "This is thy palace where the perfumed light steals through the mist of alabaster lamps, and every air is heavy with the sighs of orange groves, and music from sweet lutes."

B. No, no, just down in the tone and point to the room with a wave of the hand, so: "This is thy palace etc."

M. Yes, oh, yes, that's [illegible] acting (Repeats lines) "This is thy palace" etc.

B. Bravo! Bravo! (Claps — to [illegible]) Why don't you clap — (stops) them. Really, my dear, I feel — hem. (to Ch.) Well sir, what are you grinning at again?

M. (Turns, sees Ch.) Oh, I did not [illegible] Mr Travers [illegible] there anything [illegible] me. (Bows ceremoniously to Ch., then turns away to Bar. confidentially) Oh! I am so [illegible] the theater, and actors — Don't you [illegible] the theater papa?

B. Eh! — yes, yes — very much [illegible] of course — you understand — [illegible] and — and [illegible].

M. Oh! I dote on acting! [illegible] convent you know we were always [illegible] plays.

B. Plays!

M. Oh, yes [illegible] splendid plays! and they always gave me the best parts (Glances [illegible])

B. (Getting excited) [illegible]!

M. (Looks back at Ch.) [illegible] born actress!

B. Ha! [illegible] you are! [illegible]!

M. They said it must be in my [illegible].

B. (Claps [illegible]) [illegible] to the core! [illegible] what will [illegible]!

End of Act I

Act I [illegible]

[illegible] this morning?

[illegible]

[illegible] of real [illegible]

[illegible] must be his [illegible]

[illegible] farmer in [illegible] this morn- [illegible] and [illegible] takes care [illegible]

[illegible] designed by nature to play the [illegible] mischief with the feminine heart, you are in luck! — Access gained to the inner works of the fort, garrison more than half won over [illegible], the very moment the little [illegible] was exposed to the archery of my eyes 'Twas all over with her — she trembled, she turned pale, she wavered in her step — I know the signs! — [illegible] there is nothing like ardor with the [illegible] sex, — throw your whole soul into your eyes! [illegible] epithets mountain [illegible] not to think, but pour out a [illegible] of passionate [illegible], and drown [illegible] in an overwhelming rush of [illegible] — Romeo! Ah! [illegible] my consign me to the [illegible] time when my soul [illegible] to the [illegible] of the tragic muse! — [illegible] I am now [illegible] Romeo! [illegible] the balcony — [illegible] — "Lady, by yonder [illegible] moon I [illegible], that tips with silver all these fruit-tree tops — — [illegible] my [illegible]. I [illegible] than [illegible]! — Ah, Juliet [illegible] well! [illegible] [illegible] [illegible] and [illegible] [illegible] [illegible] [illegible] again. [illegible] my [illegible] [illegible] [illegible] [illegible] and call [illegible] [illegible] Ringo [illegible] on talk [illegible] [illegible] a [illegible] wonder which [illegible] is [illegible] [illegible] Barry [illegible] [illegible] confounding [illegible] waiting [illegible] — How's a cure to tie which [illegible] is a wanting. — [illegible] use [illegible] manage to get on by [illegible] line and [illegible] Lena, but when I call her Miss Lena [illegible]

[illegible] tour, she turns upon me like wind [illegible] "Do you remember" she says "that my name is Miss Madeline Barry" says she. [illegible] Miss Madeline Barry they may both be so [illegible] [illegible] that minds may take their pick & turn them – which they are not my style (Miss Madeline [illegible]) – Oh, there [illegible] [illegible] miss – just gone miss.
M. [illegible]
S. Oh [illegible] – it must [illegible] Madeline [illegible]
[illegible]!
M. [illegible]?
S. [illegible]
[illegible]
[illegible]
M. [illegible]!
S. [illegible]
S. [illegible]! ([illegible] Madeline [illegible] you [illegible], points [illegible]
M. [illegible] letter?
[illegible] – oh!
[illegible]!
[illegible]!
[illegible]
[illegible]
[illegible]
[illegible]
[illegible]
right [illegible]
fixed [illegible]
M. [illegible]
[illegible].
S. [illegible]
M. [illegible]
[illegible].
S. [illegible]!
M. [illegible] –
S. [illegible]
M. [illegible]

the road seven times [illegible]

M. What impertinence!

S. No, no. What [illegible] iment, on the contrary [illegible] have seen his eyes, [illegible] [illegible] with [illegible] and [illegible] [illegible] tion and such a graceful [illegible] you have [illegible]

M. Oh, yes, I have [illegible] useful piece of machinery [illegible] perfect order [illegible] wouldn't you kind, [illegible] little [illegible] hands over [illegible]

S. Yes, [illegible] without [illegible]

M. I am afraid [illegible] wanting [illegible] with your [illegible]

S. Just wait till you [illegible]

M. Oh, [illegible] kindred soul!

S. Well, my dear, [illegible] meet our eyes [illegible]

M. Yes you [illegible]!

S. Oh! so [illegible]

M. Not [illegible]

S. Oh, no, not [illegible] I can hear [illegible] as if heaven [illegible]

M. Dear me!

S. It was [illegible] it was not [illegible] the kind before [illegible]!

M. Oh, so you [illegible]

S. Yes, dear, [illegible] not [illegible] corner [illegible] –

M. Was he [illegible].

S. Well, you may [illegible] over the grass [illegible] thrill all through me [illegible] from [illegible]

[illegible] woman

[illegible] sweet heart! [illegible]

[illegible] it is the loveliest thing

[illegible] on this eyes!

M. [illegible] it is mine - I wore it that

[illegible] from France (this is excitedly)

[illegible] & Human

[illegible]

[illegible] worn it [illegible]

[illegible] you may have it.

[illegible] ointment [illegible]

[illegible] back [illegible] - [illegible] wears.

[illegible] fire) there!

[illegible] Tims it

[illegible] rich

[illegible] for the last three

[illegible] there, and - and -

[illegible] not get so excit-

[illegible]

[illegible], and [illegible], and in-

[illegible]

[illegible] your mouth (give

[illegible] forgiven [illegible]

[illegible]

[illegible] time

[illegible] I am not

[illegible] saying)

[illegible]

[illegible] tic.

[illegible] I think

[illegible]

[illegible] to [illegible] — the fact is [illegible] have [illegible] come and may be a [illegible] weeks because of a foolish affair (laughs) with a young curate.

[illegible]. Oh, yes she told me something about it.

[illegible]. Of course she did. (laughs)

[illegible]. I wrote to you because I wanted to [illegible] you — I hope you won't think me foolish and [illegible].

[illegible]. My [illegible] [illegible]

[illegible]. [illegible] understand English [illegible] and if [illegible] wrong you must tell [illegible] [illegible] (smiles)! [illegible] to consult [illegible] professionally, as a lawyer.

[illegible]. A lawyer! [illegible] of course. — of course — [illegible] —

[illegible]. But first you must promise me that you [illegible] will mention [illegible] me —

[illegible]. Not to [illegible].

[illegible]. Especially not [illegible].

[illegible]. Oh, certainly — certainly, if you insist.

[illegible]. It is a [illegible] wish to contest.

[illegible]. A will.

[illegible]. Yes, [illegible] [illegible] will [illegible] [illegible] assure you —

[illegible] [illegible] what should [illegible] in [illegible] which [illegible] might [illegible] —

[illegible]. [illegible] you [illegible].

[illegible]. [illegible] you think I am blind.

[illegible]. [illegible] did you [illegible].

[illegible]

[illegible]

[illegible]

[illegible] [illegible] (laughs) — [illegible]!

[illegible]. [illegible] you —

[illegible] you think I [illegible], no feeling!

[illegible]. How [illegible] anxious to [illegible]

[illegible] from the knowledge
[illegible]. What is good enough for papa is good enough for [illegible] — [illegible] papa goes I'll go, [illegible] stay [illegible], I'll do — I'll be with him to help him [illegible] him —
[illegible] your father will never consent.
M. Oh, [illegible] — [illegible], oh! I [illegible] such [illegible] it [illegible], it will be such fun, [illegible] me — You see, [illegible] saying I was a French [illegible] on the stage, and then I [illegible], [illegible] [illegible] in the [illegible] down there [illegible] — in [illegible], and so [illegible].
[illegible] know you at once.
M. [illegible] wait till you see me [illegible]! [illegible] I'll never leave him [illegible] the stage [illegible], and papa.
[illegible]
M. Oh, it [illegible] — [illegible] shall be [illegible] in [illegible].
[illegible]!
M. And [illegible] you the other night — you must forgive me — I know I was angry, and I am so [illegible] tempered I hardly know what I say — and I have no doubt I was very rude to you — and it is no wonder you went away and never came near me ever since. But I [illegible] so sorry [illegible], and [illegible] won't you forgive me — (holds out her hands)
[illegible]. Forgive you — I forgive you. Oh if you knew — Madeline, if you could [illegible] know! — Madeline, can't you see — can't you understand? — [illegible] engaged to my brother. —
M. I am not.
[illegible]. He loves you —

M. Loves me! – Save me from such love! – Why, he does not even think it worth his while to take a run up to town to inspect me! (bitterly) You, at least, did me the honor to find out my utter worthlessness before you dropped me –

Ch. Madeline, you will drive me mad! Ah! can't you see? – But you are right it is better as it is – better that you should hate me – better that we should never meet – there are reasons – reasons I cannot explain why you and I should be as strangers –

M. Strangers – you and I as strangers!

Ch. Madeline, I cannot explain – you would not understand – as you say, you do not know English [illegible] – little things which to an English girl [illegible] mean nothing – to you – with your French notions – might seem –

M. Charles! – Mrs Bowers – I do not [illegible] –

Ch. No, no, that's it, [illegible] the other night – I was imprudent – I was wrong. –

M. Wrong?

Ch. Not as when a girl is [illegible] –

M. [illegible] – I [illegible] understand you – the other night you and I sitting [illegible] the [illegible] – even according to English [illegible] – I was wrong!

Ch. No no –

M. And yet you allow [illegible] you [illegible] – my [illegible] – you, [illegible] my father had [illegible] – you knew [illegible] it was wrong, and you let me! – Oh [illegible] shame!

Ch. Madeline, there was no wrong –

M. Oh, now I see it all – your sudden change – your coldness and your [illegible] – you thought I had gone too far – you feared I might [illegible] a victim perhaps – Good Heavens! are you a [illegible] – a student of the human heart so dull that a school girl must tell you that were she heart stricken by your charms she would hardly laugh and [illegible]

[illegible] by your [illegible] in name! – And now, this letter of mine calling you here – forcing you to break your prudent resolve not to expose me again to the awful danger of meeting you! (Laughs) Oh, shame, shame! (falls on chair with face in her hands and sobs violently)

Ch. Madeline Oh, Madeline – What shall I do? – what shall I say? – How make you understand – Oh, forgive me!

M. Forgive you? – For what? – For wishing to spare me? – for giving me due warning – before my poor heart is quite gone? (Laughs) Rather should I thank you (Points to Barry who enters) But I will bid my father thank you in my name. (Enter Barry)

B. [illegible] at it again! always quarrelling –

M. Not at all, I was just thanking Mr [illegible], and so must you papa, for his [illegible] care lest my too susceptible [illegible] should go astray.

[illegible]

B. [illegible] nonsense – you'll drive the boy mad [illegible] what the devil are you doing here?

M. Oh, [illegible] is not to blame – I wrote to him – I asked [illegible] – think of it! are you not horrified [illegible]?

Ch. [illegible]

M. [illegible] express my thanks (Exit)

Ch. [illegible] stand it –

[illegible] the matter [illegible] you been saying [illegible]

[illegible]

[illegible] her and [illegible] o'clock, half [illegible] twelve – I just [illegible] Oh! by the [illegible] this

:

I [illegible] not intend to take another, [illegible] [illegible] somehow went right [illegible] [illegible] we shall be late (running [illegible] [illegible] they meet [illegible], who enters) [illegible] walking? – That's right, nothing like fresh air and exercise (kisses her) to bring the [illegible] in a girl's cheeks – We must hurry off [illegible] (Exeunt)

[illegible] (much excited) Dear me! how my heart beats – I knew he was following me – he [illegible] any moment (calls) Madeline [illegible] (runs and opens door) Madeline! [illegible] I have just seen him again!

M. [illegible] ought to be ashamed –

[illegible] Oh, don't say a word – don't speak – (mysteriously) He followed me all round the park [illegible] [illegible] my existence!

[illegible] Oh, no, no – he was most respectful.

[illegible] What he addressed you!

[illegible] Oh no, no – he only bowed – but such a bow – such a grand air – Madeline I am sure he is some nobleman, who – who not [illegible]

M. Nonsense – (Enter Servant with card)

[illegible] Oh!

[illegible] That's him, that is – [illegible] was him before.

[illegible] [illegible] [illegible] [illegible]

M. (reading) [illegible]

[illegible] (anxiously) [illegible] [illegible]

M. I'll not see him. (to Serv.) Tell the gentleman Miss Barry is out.

Ser. He [illegible] Miss Barry [illegible] asked for, mum.

M. I'll not see him – I'll not see any one.

[illegible] [illegible] [illegible] coming all the way from Oxford.

M. [illegible] call on you

[illegible] But Madeline, you can't mean it – you [illegible] [illegible] [illegible] – He saw me coming in, & [illegible] [illegible] [illegible] & must insist (Steps [illegible]) [illegible] Miss Barry will be most happy.

[illegible] [illegible] (Exit)

[illegible] Then you'll have to receive him [illegible] [illegible] away) [illegible] My dear Madeline.

[illegible] If you are so taken with his looks [illegible] Oh, Lena! if you [illegible] only fall in love!

[illegible] then you!

[illegible] your endless blessings upon [illegible] bowing head

[illegible] will ask for you —

M. He will ask for Madeline Barry! — [illegible] well as mine — Oh, Lena, [illegible]

[illegible] darling [illegible]

[illegible] divine [illegible]

[illegible]

[illegible] of the [illegible]

[illegible]

[illegible]

Lov. Uncle – uncle? bah! (snaps fingers) this [illegible] his objections.

[illegible] He might try to interfere –

Lov. We must baffle him.

J. Edward!

Lov. Can you trust me?

J. How can you ask?

Lov. With anything?

J. Try me.

Lov. Then this very day our destinies must be indissolubly linked – all is ready –

J. Oh, I shall faint –

Lov. Heroic girl be firm – at three o'clock a carriage will await you at the corner of the street.

J. Oh, I never can –

Lov. Then all is lost.

J. I will be there.

Lov. 'Tis well – but we must have some sign some token to prevent all mistake – a glove [illegible] ribbon – something that you will know at once

J. This (takes off ribbon, gives it to him) Oh, Edward

Lov. The very thing! (kisses it – puts it in his hat) This token will flutter from the carriage, I will [illegible] there to receive you – we drive off – I have a special licence ready prepared – we stop [illegible] church – the clergyman waits – in a [illegible] the indissoluble knot is tied – and [illegible] cast ourselves at your father's feet and implore his blessing! – –
[illegible] (opens his arms)

J. [illegible] (They embrace)

Lov. [illegible] – we have no time to lose [illegible] steps on the stairs – go sweet[illegible], go – not a word of this to a living soul – [illegible] mystery (kisses hand – Exit [illegible] assumes a rollicking air, puts [illegible] as Charles enters) Tol. [illegible] – Hullo! – Hullo! – why [illegible] my B[illegible] that you?

[illegible]

[illegible] waiting for old Blunderbuss

Sit down - don't mind me - make yourself at home - .

Ch. That is what you seem to be doing
with a vengeance. [breaks out] d— your
impudence!

Fov. See here, young man - do you know
whom you are speaking to? [illegible] himself [illegible] - What kind of language is that
for a good little boy to use? [groans] Would
you disgrace your honorable calling and
[illegible] respectable parents?

[illegible], enough of this tomfoolery.

[illegible] foolery sir. - Does it make up
[illegible] tomfoolery, sir? [illegible] his
collar [illegible] vamp, corned [illegible] cormorant! I [illegible]
the most! Learn sir that I count as low
trifling are divorced for ever - Henceforth
my genius soars to higher realms - Shakespeare sir - the divine William, and the higher realms of the modern drama!

Ch. Come, come [illegible] no [illegible] more
What are you up to here?

Fov. Well, I say I like that - What can [illegible]?

Ch. I'll tell you what - you'll have to leave
this room.

[illegible] the [illegible] me - who
[illegible]

[illegible] if it [illegible]

[illegible] I just [illegible] your [illegible] attitudes
[illegible] who first
[illegible]

Ch. [illegible] I'll have no
[illegible] with Bur-
[illegible] He don't
[illegible]

Fov. [illegible] you know [illegible] I am
[illegible] He wants
[illegible] family
[illegible] beloved, [illegible] cat,
[illegible] himself [illegible]
[illegible]

Ch. (Angry) Come, stop this (approaches)
[illegible] Madam! Look out! (puts up his back and
spits like a [illegible] Sh-r-r - Sh-r- (charges on Ch.
spitting and [illegible] at him with his cane) Sh-r-r!
Ch. [illegible] (snatches cane, breaks it and
throws [illegible] pieces - Lovel's hat falls off)
Lov. [illegible]! - Hello! - Confound you! (runs after
his cane) A five shilling [illegible] (picks up pieces)
I say, there's no joke - destroying a [illegible] Lovel's
property - (puts pieces together) you'll just
[illegible] this cane -
Ch. [illegible] smooth
[illegible] up ribbon
[illegible] it) Oh,
[illegible] get you [illegible] - that go away
- I am not [illegible] today - that's a good fellow
go - [illegible] Lov. - is about to put ribbon
[illegible] That's fine! the ribbon -
Lov. [illegible] you know -
Ch. [illegible] you the right! - How have you!
[illegible] this is just joking you know
[illegible] ribbon) Come - come -
Ch. [illegible] you this! [illegible]! You
[illegible]!
Lov. [illegible]
[illegible]
Ch. - You [illegible] it!
Lov. [illegible] - all right, my [illegible]
her own [illegible] - (laughs)
Ch. Scoundrel, [illegible]! (Lov. [illegible]). Go!
go - I would do no violence [illegible] - I'll return
this to Miss Fanny myself - (in great excitement)
[illegible]! - or I'll do that we'll [illegible] for
life - I am dangerous! - go [illegible] - go -
(Lov. backs to door as curtain [illegible])

End of Act II.

Act III

Barry's rooms in Seymour Street – Table covered with plays etc – theatrical pictures, bills etc on walls – Charles sits at table studying a part.

Ch. (Recites) "And if we have raised an innocent smile, or caused a gentle tear –" (throws down book) Oh, trash! – How I do hate these appeals to the public – (takes book) I'll never know this part – I hate the whole thing – it [illegible] hollow pretense! – Bah! it's no worse [illegible] than all the stage – Deception, lies and [illegible]! – I'll leave this place – I'll go to Australia and raise sheep – then at least when I gaze in their dull honest eyes will mean no lies. (Enter B.)

B. Oh, you here –

Ch. Yes, I was trying to get this part.

B. (Looks at clock) Why, it's about time our little friend were here.

Ch. And about time I should be gone.

B. I don't know how it is but there is something about that child's letter that [illegible] me [illegible]. I suppose I have a soft spot here for every girl on my darling's account.

Ch. I hope you'll have every reason to be satisfied with your new pupil, sir (going) Oh, there is a letter for you (goes back to desk) [illegible] from Ned.

B. Ah, it is about time we heard [illegible] from him – (feels in his pockets then [illegible] [illegible]) You'll have to read it [illegible] my [illegible].

Ch. (reads) "My dear uncle" –

B. I suppose he'll explain what he has [illegible] me [illegible]

Ch. (reads) "Yours of the 20th [illegible] Madeline's photo [illegible]"

B. I hate these commercial forms – well, go on –

Ch. (reads) "She is charming" –

B. I should think so

Ch. (reads) "and I [illegible] written before had I not been [illegible] expecting, an event which I must say places me in a strange dilemma –"

B. H'm, when I was a young fellow – but go on, go on

Ch. (reads) "You must know that I have just [illegible]…

given a fellowship

[illegible] Edward a fellow. Hurrah! Ha. [illegible] I told you the boy would make [illegible].

Ch. (reads) [illegible] is worth three hundred a year but [illegible] could not hold if married!"

B. That's so – you know these fellowships have to be resigned when a man marries – that is so – I never [illegible] of that – Well, well, what of that, [illegible] glory of getting it – What's a [illegible] three hundred! Pshaw! They'll do very well without it – I'll double his allowance! – go on –

Ch. (reads) [illegible] course if you [illegible] insist upon it, I will resign [illegible] fellowship [illegible]"

[illegible] Read [illegible] – If I insist –

[illegible] upon it, I will resign!" –

[illegible] I insist – Good heavens! What does [illegible] mean? Go on, why don't you go on?

[illegible] Master [illegible] I have never met [illegible] think it would be more prudent!" –

[illegible] the scoundrel! the hound! (Snatches [illegible] and [illegible] it under foot) the white [illegible] dastard! "Insist upon it!" [illegible] dead! –

[illegible] Mr. B[illegible] will be easily consoled

[illegible] never – never! If I [illegible] scoundrel's gown from [illegible] disown [illegible] (takes his hands) [illegible] a profession – [illegible]

[illegible]

[illegible] now – I [illegible] ster's two [illegible] more I [illegible] ate – but [illegible] ngest of my [illegible] just break- [illegible] I am so glad [illegible] – You'll

[illegible]
[illegible] to [illegible] [illegible]
[illegible]
[illegible]
[illegible] that [illegible] you, [illegible]
you [illegible] in his [illegible]
[illegible]
[illegible]
[illegible]
[illegible]
[illegible]

[illegible]
[illegible] you
[illegible]
[illegible]
[illegible]
[illegible]
[illegible]
[illegible] know your
[illegible] in which you
[illegible]
[illegible]
[illegible] have
[illegible]
[illegible]
[illegible]
[illegible]
[illegible] wife
[illegible] the girls,
[illegible]
[illegible] with a
[illegible] tell.
[illegible] mad?
[illegible] to
[illegible]
[illegible] motive
[illegible] a profession has so many
[illegible] especially for a woman [illegible]
[illegible]
[illegible] for [illegible]

[illegible] very [illegible] reward.

[illegible] my child, for [illegible] must [illegible] yourself. [illegible] many temptations [illegible] most innocent [illegible]

[illegible]

W. [illegible] scene—

[illegible] days for [illegible]

[illegible] the beam [illegible]

B. [illegible] is one of [illegible] my laughing, my dear, that [illegible] ambitions. [illegible] Sister is one of my [illegible]

M. [illegible] very [illegible]

you [illegible] laughing [illegible] me.

B. No, no, no — [illegible] — [illegible]

[illegible] see [illegible]

must [illegible]

you [illegible]

[illegible]

[illegible]

[illegible]

[illegible] — Now [illegible]

[illegible] — good [illegible]

[illegible]

[illegible]

this [illegible]

[illegible]

[illegible]

M. ([illegible]) [illegible]

[illegible]

have [illegible]

in [illegible]

B. [illegible]

out — [illegible]

Well, [illegible]

have [illegible]

M. "Authori[illegible]

authority [illegible]

[illegible]

B. Now [illegible]

loss of your [illegible]

as you [illegible]

and mind [illegible]

[illegible]

[illegible]

— and I [illegible]

my [illegible]

can [illegible]

[illegible]

[illegible]

[illegible]

friend [illegible]

sounds [illegible]

them — if you had been [illegible]

[illegible] ; but you forget
[illegible] situation was when I married you."
N. Yes, [illegible] 'twas a very disagreeable one, [illegible] I would never have married you."
S. Ha ha [illegible] a little louder - just a little louder [illegible], that's very good. - "Yes, yes, madam, you were then in a somewhat humbler style; the daughter of a plain country squire and I have made you a woman of fashion, [illegible] of rank; in short I have made you my wife!"
N. "Well then, and there is but one thing more you can now do to add to the obligation, and that is -"
S. "My widow, I suppose, [illegible] widow!
N. H'm [illegible]
S. [illegible] - show me - with a [illegible] a conscious look. so: "H'm!
[illegible]
[illegible] H'm! -
[illegible] not quite the thing yet." H'm! - H'm!"
H'm!
[illegible]
N. [illegible], I should think you would [illegible] your wife thought a woman of taste."
S. [illegible] taste - Zounds! madam, you [illegible] you married me!"
N. [illegible], Sir Peter, and after [illegible] I should never pretend [illegible] - ha -"
[illegible] bravo, bravo!
[illegible] little teaching [illegible] hand) From [illegible] my pupil,
[illegible]
[illegible] here - Sir [illegible] fall upon [illegible]
[illegible]
[illegible] will study [illegible] secrets"

of my art — the experience and study of a life time! — I will show you how to express every feeling and passion of the human soul! — Here, see — (makes a face) What does this express?

M. (Perplexed) What?

B. Yes, yes (repeats face)

M. Oh! dread —

B. No, no, joy! That was joy — estatic joy! And now this! (makes another face)

M. Oh, that was hate —

B. (throws up his arms) Hate! — Why, that was love! wild passionate love! — But it takes time and study to understand such things — It is like the higher regions of esthetic art — Mr Whistler's pictures for instance, his nocturne in black and gold or his arrangement in brown.

M. Oh, I will study so hard!

B. I know you will — ha, ha! we will show the British public what is meant by true acting! (Enter Charles)

Ch. Oh, pardon me, I thought you were alone — (draws back.)

B. No, no, come in — come in — I want you here.

Ch. No, excuse me.

B. (Pulls him in) I want you to see her — ha, ha! my boy, we are made up now. (enthusiastically — points to Mad.) Beagle to my Sir Peter! — Juliet and Pauline to your Romeo and your Claude! — We'll star the provinces! Here — here, I must see you act together — (seizes play books — selects one) this little scene in Bulwer's Money —

Ch. You'll have to excuse me, sir — the lady is no doubt a most perfect actress — but —

B. What! tut, tut, tut! don't tell me (forces book into Madeline's hand) Just this one little scene — not a dozen lines, here —

M. (draws back) [illegible], no —

B. (forces book in his hand) There. I'll not be

Aside
Ch. Oh, I have rehearsed with this lady before.
J. What?
Ch. Yes, it was a new play - A man meets with a girl, and bewitched by what he takes to be the sweet freshness of guileless innocence he loves her - loves her so that the flame burns out his very soul! - yet by some arrangement in the plot, he is bound in honor to conceal his love - She sees it all, of course, and toys with his heart as a cat with a mouse - She draws him on, and on until he is on the very point of letting loose the torrent of his love - then she checks him, and for that once he succeeds in tearing himself away from the siren's toils - That is the first act.
[illegible] - [illegible]
Ch. The [illegible] was I expect - but let me tell [illegible] the second act - For a while the wretched moth succeeded in keeping away from the flame but she had not done with him yet - there was more fun to be derived from his misery - more food for her vanity in the spectacle of his degradation - She calls him back - smiles to him - and once more makes a football of his very heart - Nor is that all - while [illegible] playing fast and loose with this man, she loves another -
M. Another I -
Ch. Oh, let me relate the play to the end - she loved another, and as a pledge of her love for that other man she - the coy - the sweet - the innocent maiden - she who had never spoken to a young man alone [illegible] - she who knew nothing of life outside the walls of a convent - [illegible] gave him this! ([illegible] ribbon)
M. [illegible] no no - (Exit [illegible])
Ch. [illegible] I now return to the fortunate recipient of the lady's favor, and it to love [illegible] you know Charly - [illegible]

to [illegible], you [illegible]
be - all the same & must say your [illegible]
away that piece of property - However [illegible]
out his hand) wish me joy -
Ch. With all my heart (wrings his hand)
B. (Who has looked on in bewilderment) What in
the name of nonsense do you all mean?
Ch. (to Mad.) Allow me to congratulate you.
Gov. Well, it means - The fact is, that [illegible]
you were a telling me about the [illegible] Don -
B. Don't mention that fellow to me sir! - The
contemptible, cold blooded, miserable sneak!
I would not have him for a son of mine
the vile calculating - - d - the Don, [illegible]!
Gov. Oh! with all my heart - d - the Don!
d - the Don! Hurrah! - - and now that
the Don is disposed of I may as well tell
you at once, that your lady [illegible]
and I (clasps his [illegible], [illegible]!
they fall at Barry's feet) - Bless us, father!
Lena. Oh, bless us!
Gov. (Aside) [illegible]
tableau!
B. Lena! well, [illegible], this is [illegible]
but you are a good kind [illegible]
Well, well (Shakes Gov's hand [illegible]
Take good care of her [illegible]
Ch. Lena! Oh! - (turns [illegible]
explaining and [illegible])
B. Well, there is one comfort [illegible]
Madeline will never leave [illegible]
M. (Aside) Never [illegible]
ed sorrow) [illegible]
and - and you [illegible]
B. Want you! Why, [illegible]
have two daughters
M. No - I can brook no rival in my father's
heart - I [illegible] it all - [illegible]
else act with him [illegible]
and care for him (falls in his arms) father!
B. Oh! -

M. [illegible] me - your Madeline - your child!
[illegible]. Madeline -
Lov. Madeline! - What! How! but Madeline is here -
Ch. Yes, [illegible] Madeline -
B. What! So he thought - ha ha ha ha But not my Madeline (Puts hand on Lov.'s shoulder) "Oh, Joseph, Joseph" (points to Ch.) He'll be a "Bishop first"
Lov. Confound it! (Checks himself and takes Lena's hand) I am satisfied; if he is to be a Bishop I'll be an Archdeacon.
B. That's right - all's well that ends well. Charly, my boy (takes his hand) Where is Madeline? (takes her hand, puts it in Charle's)
M. (Start[illegible]) No, no -
Ch. ([illegible]ingly) Madeline -
M. Mr Travers has become a woman hater - "heartless coquettes, who toy with a man's heart as a cat with a mouse" who "make a foot ball of - -
Ch. Have you no mercy!
M. Besides Mr Travers has just informed me of his intention of leaving the stage, and as I am going to be an actress -
B. You! - I'd like to see you!
M. So you will, papa - Oh, I have your promise - I am to be your pupil - "your very ow[n]" "Teazle to your Sir Peter" -
Ch. [illegible] "Juliet to my Romeo!"
M. Well, if papa should cast me in the part [illegible]
[illegible] must be, must be! - Here Charly, stand [illegible] her side - we two will take care [illegible] - A [illegible] actress! How dare you miss!
M. [illegible] papa - you know it is in my [illegible].
B. I [illegible] the child is right she is just a - -
Ch. [illegible] Block!

End of act III.